BLACK VS WHITE

Who will win this war

JIMMY JAYAN J

INDIA • SINGAPORE • MALAYSIA

ISBN
Paperback 979-8-89588-345-7
Hardcase 979-8-89744-590-5

Chapter 1

Love

A military system of a beautiful kingdom. That country's name is White. White is beautiful and a small kingdom in nature. A new major came to the White Kingdom. Now, he goes to the king's room to see the king. The king's name is Lord Kajakodaki.

Rail said himself:

"I am so late. What should I do?"

A shadow was following the major Rail work, but he didn't know about that. The king, Lord Kajakodaki, goes to the town of – Ko to see the swordsmith. Rail is now at the main door of the king's room. Rail said:

"Good morning, Lord Kajakodaki."

But there was a cute girl sitting on the Kajakodaki chair. That girl said to Rail: "Mr Rail, you're so late."

"Who are you?"

"Shut your mouth."

Jov came to the Kajakodaki's room and covered the mouth of Major Rail. That cute girl is the sister of Lord Kajakodaki. We call her the queen. Queen Neel. Jov is the top mansabdari of the White Kingdom. Mansab is a military system. You know, the White Kingdom is the world's biggest kingdom. Lord Kajakodaki came to the Gyro Mansion. The Gyro Mansion is the mansion of Kajakodaki.

Rail, Qneel, and Jov are now at Gyro Mansion. Kajakodaki

Came to his room. You know Qneel and Lord Kajakodaki have a soft heart. The military system is very strong. Kajakodaki had a soft heart, but when he became angry, he became so powerful. And came to the track when Kajakodaki came to the room, major Mr. Rail said to Lord Kajakodaki: "Good morning, Lord Kajakodaki," and Kajakodaki said to Rail: "Hey, Mr. Rail Vork, you're the next and new major of our White Kingdom. So please follow our rules. Then I went with you once to teach you some things. His name is Rook. Rook Ode." In the Kajakodaki room, there was a photo on the table. Rail saw the photo, and Rail said: "Who is in the photo, Mr Rook?" Rook said to major Mr Rail: "On the right side is Lord Kajakodaki, on the left side is Qnell and the middle is the father of Lord Kajakodaki and Qnell."

Rail said to Rook, "I think there's a big story behind the history of the White Kingdom."

Then Rook said to Rail: "Yes, there was a big story behind the White Kingdom. Do you know about the White Kingdom? Please tell me that story." That time, Jov came to the room and said: "Hey guys, I disturbed you." Next, Rook said: "No, Mr Monkey. Who is the villain of our story?"

"The slave! BLOOD the devil's."

The

devil.

The

devil.

The

devil.

The

devil.

The

devil.

The blood

The blood killed the sister of San Death, the king of the Black Kingdom.

Chapter 2

Who is Raih and San Death

The color black isn't a beautiful color. But the black kingdom is very beautiful. The last wall and the city of butterflies are a little different. But the devil came, and the beauty became blank. The blood of the slave!!!!!!!!!!!!!!!!. San Death is going to marry the princess of the White Kingdom, Qneel, and the princess of the black kingdom, Qraih, is going to marry the lord of the White Kingdom, Kajakodaki. But the devil came to the wedding and kidnapped Qraih. Then, the next day, Blood kills Qraih and sends the dead body to the Lightning country. Blood went to the Lighting Country and wrote "rest in peace" on paper, then passed the paper to the grave of Qraih. And he smiled with a khatana.

Blood's target is Qneel. The father of San Death. Sand Death is thought to be the father of Lord Kajakodaki. Lord Syymaki killed the daughter of the Lord Sand Death. Qraih. But Lord Syymaki is innocent in this case. A big conflict started between the White Kingdom and the black kingdom. Sand's death and San's death killed Lord Syymaki. At that time, Jack killed Lord Sand Death. Next, San Death killed Jack and ran away. The bond between the White Kingdom and the black kingdom broke. The revenge of San Death became very big. But Lord Kajakodaki didn't have any revenge against San Death.

Chapter 3

Are You Ready

One week later, the Rail said: "What a job! I am so tired. Now, I wish to become a king like Lord Kajakodaki."

"Major Mr Rail, we have a mission. Nature is attacked. A crystal attacked a Markey mansion in Water Country. Come on fast, we have a mission. The Yellow Kingdom came to the White Kingdom to ask for help. They are poor. They say help them to defeat a demon. My brother went to Artisum village."

The devil

Blood came to the White Kingdom

to defect Lord Kajakodaki.

Chapter 4

The Clane Death

The clan death is the second strongest clan in the world. The secret weapon of the clan is death. San Death is the seventh mass of the Death Clan. Jyro is the strongest man in the Death Clan. Jyro is the sense of San Death. Jyro is the third man, and he also knows about

Sayo

Sayama

Chapter 5

Power of Jov

Jov was born like a king. He had a small family. Joel, Jul, Jack, and Juroki. Juroki is so powerful and intelligent. Jack is the father of Jov. He is a Jyko master; his clan is Vork. Jul is the sister of Jov. Now, Jov is gone to kill a crystal Ramz. Jov defeats the crystal. But the slave came again! Ash, the slave, came and killed Jov. The happiness ends. The smell of blood spreads in the air. Ash is the owner of Red Crystal. **I PLEDGE MY OPINION. HE IS ALSO A SLAVE.**

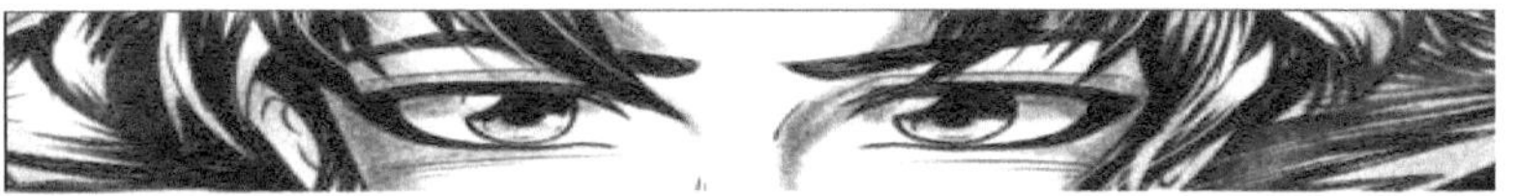

Jov isn't a bad man. Jov is a good man.

Chapter 6

In

Now, San Death is going to the White Kingdom. He went to kill Kajakodaki and cleanse the strongest kingdom in the world. I talked about the White Kingdom. But San Death didn't know. Now, Kajakodaki is so powerful. San Death didn't know Kajakodaki also knew SAYO SAYAMA. But the funny thing in this case is that death also involves SAYO SAYAMA. But he didn't use it. Mr Rails, the major, and Kajakodaki know the war is useless. But only hear the words of Kajakodaki. Kajakodaki only hears the words of the God Outsuki.

Outsuki is the first grandfather of Lord Kajakodaki.

Lighting is the nature of Lord Outsuki. But he knows 3 natures without lighting. Total Lord Outsuki knows 4 natures, and he is very powerful. He is the father of SAYO SAYAMA. We call him the Lightning God.

But on the other side, Qneel went to the swordsmith to repair her sword. Qneel went to Kawalsuki's mansion. Kawalsuki's is the world's best and most popular costly swordsmith's mansion. Qneel said, "Make a sharp and shiny sword in the universe." Kawako made a sword and gifted it to Qneel. And the war started.

Chapter 7

The Short Story of Blood

Blood is the slave of Sand Death. Blood's full name is Blood Eater. Blood's heart is made upon stone. He doesn't like the friendship between Lord Syymaki and Lord Sand Death. Outsuki's daughter is the mother of Kajakodaki; her name is Terlin. Sand Death and Lord Syymaki have a very strong friendship bond. Blood didn't like this friendship. Blood kidnaps and kills the sister of Sand Death, Qraih. Blood is the most powerful devil, but he is scared of Lord Kajakodaki. He is on Laxekoclane, but he is so powerful. He killed Terlin in his 16th year, and he killed God Outsuki in his 8th year. He joined Laxeko in his 12th year; he could defeat a country with his one finger.

The blood is the student of the white nail. We call him master. He also knows Sayosayama. He is San's grandfather, the father of sand. He also has a big brain. He knows the names of all the clans, powers, and crystals. He knows thousands of powers and obtains them. He is also godlike, our sun. Blood plans to clean the clan of Kajakodaki.

Chapter 8

A War of Vork and the History

Rail enters Kajakodaki's room. And Kajakodaki says a war started in viooleet kingdom. Rail doesn't think of going to violent kingdom*:

"What do you, Lord Kajakodaki?"

"Rook doesn't think about Rail. Rook, you know about Rail; he is the son of Juroki."

"You talk about Jov's mother, Juroki."

Jov's father, Jack's wife, is Juroki. Yes, Jov and Joel are the brothers of Rail. Rail Vorkjov and brothers are in Vork clane. Vork is a powerful clan. The weapon of the Vork Clane is so powerful and painful.

Jack Vork

|

Jovvork

|

Rail Vork

|

Joel vork

|

Jul vork

Chapter 9

The Mega Power Crystal

You know the crystal of ramz.in this world, a hundred crystals are the. In this list of crystals, we call 10 crystals gods. Godc means mega-powered crystals. The Lord Kajakodaki's crystal is

Black

Black Is The Crystal Of Lord Kajakodaki.

Name of died crystal	Owner of Crystal
juraieee	Orokilaima
Raiva	Joel
faiva	cane
laiva	blood
fortain	Raih
raila	Rail
White crystal	Ramz

This Is A List Of Deceased Crystals.

Name of godc	Owners of godc
Lighting blade	laigama
Jul	vuyuki
Qneel	dilamo
Kajakodaki	black
Qraih	Rain
San	smile
sand	sand
Blood	Blood

1st

The Gate

has Opened.

The story of Ten Crystals

Chapter 10

The Story of Lighting Blade's Crystal

Once upon a time, a child was born in a Lightning country. That child's clan is lightning. The father of that child gave the name to his son as a Lightning Blade. Once a day, Lightning Blade goes to a forest. He spends a lot of time in that forest. But he didn't know the forest's owner was Laigama. He sees a creature. The name of the creature is Laigama. The nature of Laigama is lightning. This is the most powerful crystal in the 5 countries. He can destroy the full universe like Kajakodaki. But he had a soft and loving heart. The Lightning Blade is the heart of Laigama. When Laigama came, the life of the Lightning Blade became stronger. In this world, only 5 mega natures are the 5 mega natures.

Lightning

Fire

Nature

Water

And Lightning Blade told his father about Laigama. Lightning Blade's father was Lightning Red. Lightning Red asked some questions to Laigama. Laigama answered the questions to Lightning Red. Lightning Red asked questions like, "Do you like to live in the heart of my son, Lightning Blade." Laigama gave permission to seal Laigama to the heart of Lord Lightning Blade. And Lightning Red sealed Laigama to the heart of Lord Lightning Blade. This is the story of the Crystal of Lightning Blade. Now, the father of Lightning Blade was killed in a war, and Lightning Blade became the king of Lightning country.

Chapter 11

The Story of Rain

Rain is a monster, but the heart of rain is poor and so soft. Rain is the crystal of Raih. In the rainy season, San and Raih went on an outing. At that time, Raih lost her way home. He found a cave she entered and saw a creature she called Crystal Rain. San Death came and sealed rain to the heart of Raih. At that midnight, Rih became scared. Raih consoled rain Raih is not a monster. But Raih is a monster. That night, they became friends. At that time, Raih didn't have any power like his brother, San Death. And rain lives in the heart of Raih.

Chapter 12

We Call the Real Monster as Sand Monster

Sand monster is one of the real monsters. The hobby of the sand monster is killing people with blood, but one day, Lord Syymaki seals the sand monster in the body of Lord Sand Death with the permission of Lord Sand Death. Then, Sand Death became the owner of a deathly crystal. A deathly crystal means an ugly creature who does nothing but cruelty to everyone. When that ugly creature came into Lord Sand Death's life, his life was ruined. When the creature came, who did only cruelty to all those ugly people, Lord Sand Death also started committing atrocities in his life. The sand monster kills the 3 daughters of Vuyuki, the second most powerful crystal in the universe. The sand monster has revenge on Vuyuki, and Vuyuki also has a sweet revenge on the devil crystal sand monster.

Sand Death and sand monster kill the 3 daughters of Vuyuki.

Raiva is the first victim of the sand monster. Faiva is the second victim of the sand monster. Laiva is the last victim of the sand monster.

Chapter 13

Why We Call that Crystal as Black

Black.

Why do we call this crystal a mega crystal? This is the answer to the question.

The crystal had a

soft heart

But the crystal

killed 108,96980

Monsters.

This is the answer to the question. When black loses his control, black kills his own friend. Kajakodaki is a friend of black, but the black didn't kill Kajakodaki, their very best friend.

In the middle of the night of June, all are enjoying the success of their part in the black kingdom. At that time, 2 devils escaped from the black kingdom, and they went to the blue lake in the Lightning country. Blood started a new life in the Lightning country.

Chapter 14

Vuyuki Inata's Vuyuki

Vuyukiinata's grand grandfather is the creator of the Inata clan. Inata is the most popular clan in the universe.

blood

rain

You think, what do you mean by blood rain? Blood rain is a war. The war between Blood and Jul. The result of that war is a tie.

Blood used his full power to defeat Jul. But Blood didn't know how powerful Jul Vork was. You can think Jul Vork had a crystal; the name of the crystal is Vuyukiinata. Now, Blood has become more powerful and stronger than Lord Kajakodaki. Vuyuki's real name is Icno Inata. The name of Icno's mother is Vuyuki Inata. Vuyuki, the mother of Icno Inata, was killed by Blood. That's so. Icno changed his name to Vuyukiinata. Vuyuki wishes for the death of Blood.

Chapter 15

Smile

You know, the king of the black kingdom, San Death, has a crystal called,

Smile

Every time and every situation, the crystal smile and smile. The power of a smile is a smile. A smile is also a smile. A smile is good. It's like Kajakodaki.

Smile

Smile

smile

Smile

Smile

Smile

His power is also

Smile

This is some information

about Smile

Chapter 16

Why Dilamo?

The Qneel have a crystal named 'dilamo'. Dilamo is the slave of X. X is the king of all crystals. Qneel recovered dilamo from the slavery of X. All the crystals call X Lord king. But Vuyuki is the real boss. X is the servant of Vuyuki. But the legend is Laigama. Laigama is the strongest crystal; he never dies. The birth of Qneel is a surprise. On her 6th birthday, Kajakodaki gifts the crystal dilamo and seals dilamo into the stomach of Qneel. This is the first of our

DILAMO.

And Qneel and dilamo became friends and now dilamo lives in the heart of Qneel. The real name of dilamo is

Diamond Illlsuyukiinata

Yes, "Dilamo or diamond ill suyukiinata 'sclane is inata the first owner of dilamo is Natasha laig."

There was a picture on a page. I know you saw the picture. Now, who is in the picture? This is the answer to the question. That is the picture of X, the king of 9 crystals. His hobby is selling the crystals for money. He wishes to kill the godly Lightning Blade. But he didn't know how powerful Lightning Blade and Laigama are. The war has started.

2nd

Gate is opened

The War of Mega Crystals

There are 3 fights started

between Jul and blood

Sainago vs. Blood

Lightning Blade vs. Blood

This is the 3 mega god fights

Chapter 17

Sainago vs. Blood

"S...lade wing

Blood aide

art."

"Blood.......... You my enemy, now I will bury you."

"Change the name and say this at the front of the

Crystal Lake EERE.... I WILL KILL YOU."

"BURYING DEATH CLAN."

"BLUE Ink Lake."

Blood vs Sainago is not a fight; it is a war and the story of surviving. We call Sainago as lord. You know, in that fight, Sainago.

"Snake nail punch SAYO SAYAMA."

But blood is so stronger than

'Sainago poison

Sayo

Sayama'.

Sainago uses a vibrant

necklace "Vibrant

Necklace

Show

your

Power."

Blood say:

"What the hell are you doing? I will bury you destroyer."

Gaya Lovathijinjalothi Blue Salan.

The end

Chapter 18

Lighting Blade vs. Blood

Years ago, Blade, now 21 years old and Blood now 26. This is a mass fight against Blood. Blood goes to kill Iran, in that time Blade stops Blood. Blood became angry. The first fight started. In that fight, Blood wins, but in the second fight, Blade wins. In the third fight, Blood also wins. Then in the fourth fight. Now you think Blood will win, but Blood quits and runs away, then Blade becomes the **Winner**

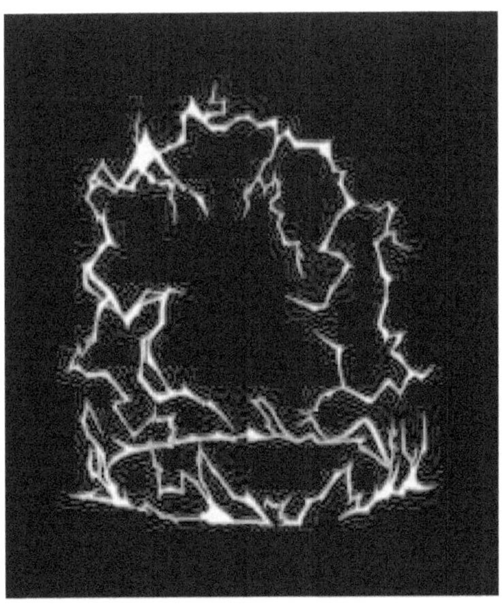

What is the reason for that defect of blood? Now, the blood and Blade are the 2 sides of one coin. But the real hero came to kill blood. The queen of the universe

Jul Vork

Came to kill the slave blood. They miss blood. Blood escapes from the Yoricho.

Chapter 19

Jul Vork vs Blood Eater

In 2 days after the fight of Blade and blood, the next fight started.

Jul vork

Vs.

Blood.

Jul easily defeats blood. The next day Jul was involved in a fight. That time is not a fight it is a war between July and blood. In the 2 days blood became stronger. He studies the ultimate magic. Jul is also stronger. This fight is known as longer. The reason for this name is because most fights are between July and blood. Jul vs. blood fight is the longest fight in the 5 countries.

The end

3rd

The Gate is opened

The war between

Black and White.

Chapter 20

A War

Attack

One year later, *on* a bad morning, *San* Death suddenly attacked *Kajakodaki* and White Kingdom. At that time, *Kajakodaki* was in his room. Lord Kajakodaki was talking to *Qneel* when an owl delivered a letter. The letter said

Good morning Lord

Kajakodaki And Qneel. You

Two are in a Big Problem.

The letter was received from the king of the Black Kingdom, Lord San Death. San Death came to the room of Lord Kajakodaki and said, "You're my enemy, Kajakodaki!"

That time Qneel picked up his lighting style Yoricho. That time Q Neel said this to San Death.

"I will kill you." that time "Neel shut your mouth." Kajakodaki said to Qneel "This is the time to show our power." Kajakodaki says "Ok, show your power."

Kajakodaki picked up his Yoricho too and said to his Yoricho, "Yoricho, show your power to that individual," Kajakodaki said to Yoricho. That time the slave of Sand Death came to the White Kingdom. Sand Death said to Kajakodaki, "I will show you my power, a lightning giant ball." At that time, Qneel used the power of her Yoricho.

Lighting

Magic

Cutting

Yoricho

"Neel, are you crazy?"

"Sorry, my big brother," that time **blood** came to the room and said, "Hey prince San Death, I came to spread some poison to the food of Kajakodaki. And kill that Lord."

The second color war started. Kajakodaki went to the nearest window and he saw his country going to die. Kajakodaki became angry. Kajakodaki says to Qneel, "Go to our country. I will finish my job. When I can't finish my job, I will die." The fight continues. Blood uses his khatana. Qneel uses all his power to protect the White Kingdom.

In one month, now the White Kingdom became hell. Qneel sent people to the Lighting Country's headquarters. Qneel called the lighting blade to help her brother, Lord Kajakodaki. But the lighting blade is too late. The next day, San's death became tired. But blood didn't become tired; he fought with Kajakodaki in his last breath. At that time, the death of Kajakodaki shocked the White Kingdom. During that time, Qneel killed the king of the black kingdom, Lord San's death. Blood killed Lord Kajakodaki.

Chapter 21

We Call the Country as Nature

Queen Neel asks for some help from Nature Country. The 21st king of Nature Country, called Raiyee Rock, sent some ninjas from Lightning country, Team Lightning Blade. Brutosyymaki, Herileyee Rock, and Akasilaima are the teammates of Team Lightning Blade. Team Lightning Blade is going to help the White Kingdom. Team Lightning Blade left from Lightning country's headquarters. Raiyee is preparing to go to the White Kingdom sometimes later. A letter is received from Lightning Blade. The letter says,

This is the message of Lighting

Blade The theme of team is protect

White Kingdom

私はブレードに光を当てています。今、私は白の王国を守っています。しかし、今私は悲しいです、この悲しみの理由は血で殺されたカジャコダキです。そしてニール女王は黒の王国の最後の王を殺します。私はサンの死について話しています。

Chapter 22

WHITE NAIL: The Master

White nail is the essence of blood. He can summon a giant 'Jalwamo'. Jalwamo means a mega-powered clone of Vuyuki. You know Vuyuki. Vuyuki is the second most powerful crystal. At the birthday party of White nail, all the crystals joined the party, revealing their true faces. However, one crystal was absent from the party. That crystal is the crystal of blood. During the party, the second most powerful crystal, Vuyuki, gifted his half-powered clone to White nail. White nail became very happy. Half of Vuyuki's power melted into White nail's soul. After that, White nail became very powerful. But White nail's student, Blood, killed him. Blood also took Jalwamo's power from White nail. Lord Sainago took the dead body of White nail. Master White nail went to the room of Thidarama, the third king of the country.

Leaf

Leaf the wonders of the four countries

Chapter 23

The Legend of Green

Raiyee Rock. The one and only legend in the leaf. We have 5 countries called him.

No.	Name of countries
1	Lighting
2	Fire
3	nature
4	water
5	wind

The Nature Country is the slave of Heriyee rock. Heriyee rock is the woman king of the natural country. He can heal any wound. And he is so powerful. But his weakness is blood. She was scared of blood. She is queen of Earth and nature. Master White nail is the husband of Heriyee rock.

Chapter 24

Who is the Next Ruler?

Lighting cat, folic kart, granluns. They are godcic of the White Kingdom. Godcic means the selectors of the new king. Lighting cat is the main god; the second one is folic kart. And the third is gran luns. We call them lords. The lords of the White Kingdom decide the next ruler of the White Kingdom is Queen Neel and the next day Queen Neel became the next ruler of the White Kingdom. Queen Neel had a sweet revenge against San Death. In the side, blood planning to destroy the White Kingdom. But on the next side, the laiguaicalkthi came to destroy the Earth. Now you have a QUESTION: what is the meaning of laiguaicalkthi?

LAIGU AI CALKTHI

means "The LEGEND

LIKE MAIGROW LAIMA"

THE CRATER OF LAIMA

CLANE HIMA JAMACHI

THE MOTHER OF BLOOD

JAIROO

THE ENEMY OF HERIYEE ROCK

Chapter 25

The Dream at Time

Time is also so fast and so serious.

Time is very intelligent

1

2

3

4

5

Years later. Now, Neel had a daughter called Line. She is so smart and intelligent. She is more powerful than her uncle Lord K. Kajakodaki.

Chapter 26

Lord

Juke

Laig

a

laim

ai

We call Sainago as Lord. Lord is the student of Thidarama, the third king of Nature Country. You know, Master White nail and Heriyee Rock are also students of Thidarama. Lord is a type of monster like X. Lord is the king of the Snake Kingdom. He can use locked magic. That power can recover the dead body. Lord Sainago and Kayaki are 2 devils.

Chapter 27

On the Way / Time

Lord gone to kill the line. The one and only daughter of Qneel, and a big fight started in the White Kingdom. Lord didn't know about the line. Lord can't kill Kajakodaki. The line is more powerful than Lord K. Kajakodaki. The line is a jyno. Jyno means the list of powerful people like Kajakodaki, Neel, and so on. Now the war ends. Sometimes iniquity wins: but on the other side, truth will win. And I think you can wait for it.

The Truth Is Called

truth

4th

gate is opened

the 5 countries

1 lighting

2 fire

3 nature

4 nature

5 wind

Chapter 28

Lighting Country

The Lighting country is the most powerful country in the universe. The lighting blade's country is the Lighting Country. Lighting country has thousands of clans. But some of the 10 clans have some specialties. The clans like; lighting, blue spell etc, these 2 are the mega god powerful clans in the universe. This has some specialties. This is the mega powerful 10 clans in the universe.

1	Lighting
2	Blue spell
3	spell
4	Niron
5	lox
6	x **speel**
7	Z speel
8	**Z blue speel**
9	**I nogoq**
10	A speel

Lighting

Country

Is the

country Of

Lighting blade

Chapter 29

Fire

Fire is the second most powerful country in the universe. All countries call fire a hero. The reason for this talk is that the Lighting Country can't reach the problems of the people. But fire lands sitting in the center of Earth. That so, fire land can help people easily and quickly. There are only 10 clans in the legendary fire land. That 10 is not simple. It is hard. Like the Lighting Country. And the 10 clans have secret magic power. We call the 10 clans as helpers of the poor. They are so soft. The hearts are poor and soft. These are the clans of the fire country.

1	Firer xx
2	Firerexx
3	Firer xxx
4	Firere xxx
5	Firere x
6	M lava
7	Shuzekoo FFFFE
8	D IHJ $ [THE NAME OF A MONEY LOVER CLANE]
9	D = LAV
10	C = LAV XX

Chapter 30

Nature

READ THIS LETTER:

Nature is the popular green land. It doesn't have any clane. Now nature is a ghost country. We can't determine which country is natural. But it is so powerful!!!!!!!!!!!!!!

This is the symbol of nature. You don't forget nature is also powerful.

So, so, so

Powerful

Chapter 31

Water

You know someone's in our reading team; some do not know how to swim. The reason for this talk is the fear of water. Yes, in this world, water is the real

Ghost

The Water Country is as rich as the wind. They sent ninjas to protect the small and small villages. And they send the poor people to the country's water.

And some people didn't have any power but they had gold, diamonds or money, etc.... they have an opportunity. They can transform into water citizenships. That is the special thing that has water.

Chapter 32

Wind is the Slave Dynasty

Wind country is

the Slave

Country

5th

Gate Is Opened

The last way of the first

Chapter 33

Leaf: the Beginning

Brutosyymaki said to the team of lighting blades.

"Hey, we kill Ash," then Lightning Blade said Bruto Syymaki.

"Don't enjoy we kill only the death clone of Ash."

And Bruto Syymaki said to Lightning Blade, "What is the meaning of death clone?"

Lightning Blade went to explain death clone but at that time Heriyee rock came to their room and said;

"Hey team lighting blade we have a mission xx and this is a beginning," the real fight is coming soon please wait for it

....

the mega

Chapter

Chapter 34

The Madness of Aku {the evil}

Now Lightning Blade wishes to become the king of the Lighting Country. He starts his training. But he didn't have a sense. Now you think lighting blades also have a sense. You can think lighting blade only has 22. And you know about the death of Lord White Nail. The devil's blood kills Lord White Nail. Lightning Blade goes to see the devil called Aku. In Japanese, Aku means devil. Lightning Blade says to Aku to recover Lord White Nail. Aku has magical power to recover anyone after death. That is the reason everyone calls him Aku. No one knows the real name of Aku. Aku agrees to the deal but Aku has an opinion. Aku says he recovered the White nail but Lightning Blade gave his body to him. Lightning Blade agrees to the deal. Aku recovered the White nail as a death clone. At that time, Lightning Blade kills Aku. And Lightning Blade picks the heart of Aku and destroys the heart. The reason for

That action. Aku can recover him with the help of his heart and destroy the death clone. That lighting blade activates the body of white nail. At that time lighting became sad and he cried. White nail's death clone came and gave a big hug to the lighting blade. White nail asked the lighting blade, "What is the reason for recovering me? I need you to become a strong king in the Lighting Country," and white nail became the mentor of the lighting blade. The lighting blade goes to Raiyee Rock to transform white nail's death clone into real life. White nail became normal. White nail started the training of the lighting blade. First, white nail taught the lighting blade to make a death clone of others. On the first day, white nail said to control his nature chakra. In 5 days, the lighting blade completed the first task. Then white nail gave some tips to recover the death clone. White nail said,"

....

....

....

....

....

That is a big secret. Lord Outsuki, the grandfather of the lighting blade and the creator of the lighting clan and countries. And the white nail is the only one who knows how to use the recovering magic, and now the lighting blade also knows the recovering magic. The white nail teaches the lighting blade to use several of Sayo Sayama. Then the lighting blade learned to use several of Sayo Sayama.

Example: lightning Sayo-sama, poison Sayo-sama, water shark Sayo-sama, lightning current Sayo-sama. Etc... And the white nail teaches him to use the Walttriger. Lightning Blade opens his 1-dot Walttriger. Walttriger means a powerful eye. White nails have rit-ed Walttriger. In this world, there are 7 several Walttriger. I list that."

1st	lighting walttriger
2nd	rited walttriger
3rd	xdels walttriger
4th	kills walttriger
5th	dedels walttriger
6th	redo pointo
7th	oityu

Now, white nail and Lightning Blade are going to the circle forest ground in Nature Country. White nail and Lightning Blade came to that place for training. Lightning Blade opens his one-dot Walttriger but white nail also opens his 3-dot Walttriger and fights for training. In that fight, Lightning Blade's nature power and the 1-dot Walttriger's power mix. That is a beautiful stage.

The Walttriger of Lightning Blade became 4 dots and the color became lightning blue. Then Lord White Nail opened his rited Walttriger. The power of Lord White Nail became a devil power. In one punch against a Lightning Blade, Lightning Blade's soul became dead. Lord White Nail off his rited Walttriger. You think what a rited Walttriger is. Rited Walttriger is the second powerful Walttriger in the world. The first one is lightning Walttriger; it is the Walttriger of Lord Outsuki. Now you can think how powerful Lord Outsuki is. And Lord Outsuki has 12th point. Point means when Lord Outsuki opens his 1st point, his power will increase. Then Lord Outsuki opens his 2nd

Walttriger only has 5 dots. When the lord opens his 3rd point, he shows his Walttriger katana. That katana is the most powerful katana in the world. We call that katana a Walttana. The 4th is the lord opening his normal lighting Walttriger. When the 5th point became open, the lord opened his double normal lighting Walttriger, meaning the 2 eyes became Walttriger. The lord opened his 6th point, and the Lord's chakra flowing hills became powerful and bigger than others like gods. Now you think, why did Lord Outsuki become a god? That is a good question. And the answer to the question is the lord killed a god and 7 kings. When the 7th point became open, the nuetal. Nuetal means a creature; anyone who has a walt trigger, that one has a nuetal. In this world, various nuetals Lord Outsuki also has a nuetal. His name is Shizxavo, but everybody calls him Shizavo. And Lord Outsuki has 12 points. Lord Outsuki's real name is called

LORD LIGHTING OUTSUKI LAITAL LIRON

White nail and Lighting sit under a tree for rest that time. Lighting Blade asks White nail, "What is the reason for the blood defect, you, lord sense?" White nail says the answer to the question to Lighting Blade, "I lost in front of them." Suddenly, Lighting Blade asks White nail, "Why for that sense?"

?!
?!?!?!?!

"Blood is my student."

"Whaaaatt?"

"That is a big story."

"Please talk about that story."

"Ok, blood is my 4th student. He is my blood. I love him so much than others. Lightning Blade I kill the love of blood her name is June. June is beautiful."

The back

story of

white nail

THE FOUNDER OF HIKASI CLANE. HIS NAME IS UNKNOWN.HE IS THE SENSE OF WHITE NAIL. WHITE NAIL, SAINAGO AND RAIYEE ROCK ARE THE STUDENTS. WHITE NAIL IS THE BEST STUDENT OF THE TEAM. BUT THE SAINAGO IS A DEVIL. SAINAGO IS THE SENSE OF AKASI LAIMA. NOW, SAINAGO BECAME DYING. BLOOD KILL SAINAGO THE GOD OF ILLEGAL POWERS SAINAGO SEE LIKE AN OLD MAN. BUT HE ALSO THE SAYO SAYAMA. AND CAME TO TRACK. IN

WHITE NAIL'S 22nd age he his

Love to raise rock in the bridge of love. You know this bridge. This bridge is in the list of historical bridges and places. And they became senses. That so they became 2 and now raise became the new Queen of Nature Country. Then lighting blade became the student of white nail and Heriyee rock became the student of raise rock then the akasi laima became the student of sainago. Everyone SAY SAINAGO IS THE FATHER Of

AKU. WHITE NAIL MARRIAGE RAIYEE

ROCK AND HE HAVE A SON LIKE LIGHTING BLADE. BUT HE WAS KILLED BY MAIGROW LAIMA THE GHOSTLY KING OF LAIMA CLANE.

Chapter 35

24 Natures and 52 Lighting Chkra!

White nail and lighting blade walking thought in the boulder wall of 2:3. 2:3 means fire country is to Nature Country. This is a ratio math technical. They walk and walk. Lighting blade became tired and he stops walking. But white nail didn't become tired. White nail gave some magic boiled water to lighting blade. The tiredness of lighting blade ran away. And lighting blade walk very speed as he can but white nail easily defeat the grandson of Lord Outsuki. You know the Lord Outsuki trained Lord White Nail when Lord Outsuki became a king. Then white nail trained lighting blade to recreate the neutral of Lord Outsuki with his recovering magic.

Lightning Blade recreates neutral with a bloody anger smile and asks, "Lightning Lord Waltrigger, neutral Shizxavo light now," and he recreates the legend neutral lighting Shizxavo.

Lightno. Shizxavo also helps in the practice of lighting BLADE.

Now white nail, lighting blade and Shizxavo in at the hole of death. White nail asks to lighting blade and Shizxavo "This hole is called the death hole of life. Lighting blade, your grandfather Lord Lighting Outsuki hides his Walttana in this hole

That is the most powerful katana in the world. You can hold the katana. Your new mission is to

find the katana. Shizxavo will help you to find the Lord's katana." Lighting blade and Shizxavo jump to the deep hole. They pass the devoles. Devoles means a beautiful rounded place; it is very beautiful to see. In that time, they will pass the devils; you can see the niyaku. Niyaku is the most beautiful comet ever and ever. Lighting blade and Shizxavo are at the end of the hole of death. They see a door. Lighting blade looks around the door; he sees some writing. The writing says

Lighting blade touch

my heart

Lighting blade touch the heart of Lord Otsuki

Lightning Blade see the legendary katana.

The Legendary Katana

Waltana

Lightning Blade picked the legendary katana. At that time, his normal Walttriger became legendary lightning Walttriger. At that time, his dress changed, his hairstyle changed, and his attitude. He looked at Shizxavo. Shizxavo said "Lord Lightning Outsuki!" That time the soul of Lord Outsuki came and touched the face of Lord Lightning Blade with certain pride

And Lord Lightning Outsuki said, "You are the king of my country," and Lord Outsuki vanished. Then Lord Lightning's Blade came out from the hole of death. White nail saw the Lord Lightning's Blade. White nail became shocked. White nail said, "Lord Outsuki." At that time, Shizxavo said, "This is not our lightning."

"Blade, this is our Lord Lighting Blade," Lord Lighting Blade walks like a king. At that time, Lord White Nail asks, "Now you have to practice with the legendary Walttriger katana. Walttana." Then Shizxavo resolved in lighting Walttriger. Resolved means Shizxavo recovered in the Walttriger of the Lord Lighting Blade. White nail and Lord Lighting Blade went to the deep forest of the Water Country. Lord Lighting Blade's training continued. At that time, White nail received a letter from Raiyee Rock. Raiyee Rock said White Kingdom was attacked. Lord Lighting Blade doesn't think anything. Lord Lighting Blade rect Shizxavo and Lord Lighting Blade invade White nail go White Kingdom but White nail didn't go White Kingdom. White nail "I will wait for you," Lord Lighting Blade looks at White nail and smiles. Now the Lord's Lightning Blade is going to White Kingdom. You know now Lord Lighting Blade is in Water Country. There are 3 boulders the Lord had to pass. Do you know how many boulders there are in this world? There are 20 boulders in this world. Come see that.

1:2	Lighting to fire
1:4	Lighting to water
1:5	Lighting to wind
2:1	Fire to lighting
2:3	Fire to nature
2:4	Fire to water
2:5	Fire to wind
3:2	Nature to fire

3:4	Nature to water
4:1	Water to lighting
4:2	Water to fire
4:3	Water to nature
5:1	Wind to lighting
5:2	Wind to fire
5:3	Wind to nature
3:1	Nature to lighting

Chapter 36

The Legendary War

Lord Lightning Blade in the legendary kingdom of nature. Lord's Lightning Blade sees the dangerous state of the king and people in the White Kingdom. Lord Lightning Blade opens his legendary Walttriger. Lightning Walttriger. The Walttriger of Lord Outsuki. Lord Lightning Blade picks his Walttana, and a big fight starts between Lord Lightning Blade and Blood. Blood uses his mega one-hand locking magic. Lightning Blade easily defeats all magic of Blood. Finally, a comet comes and falls into the White Kingdom. Lightning Blade easily cuts the comet into 2 pieces. The Lord's Lightning Blade easily defeats the devil's Blood. Lord Lightning Blade cuts the head of Blood. But that is only a clone of Blood. Lord Lightning Blade becomes scared about White nail. Lord Lightning Blade runs to Water Country. Lord Lightning Blade sees the death body of

....

Himari Susaki, the daughter of Blood, was killed by White nail at that time. When Lightning Blade cut the head of Blood correctly, but at that time, White Nails killed Himari. That's why the blood's real soul and body became clones. White nail and Lord Lightning Blade went to the Lightning country. To see the latest king of Lightning country. Lord Lightning Blade and White nail see the legend Yukki Shazvo Onoki. Lord Lightning Blade asks Lord Yukki with a crazy smile. "This is my seat. I am the new king of Lightning country, get out of my seat," White nail said to the king of the Lightning country, Lord Yukki, "this is the grandson of Lord Outsuki. You know Lord Outsuki is the most powerful and the creator of Lightning country. His name is Lord Lightning Blade. He had the legendary katana of Lord Outsuki, Walttana. I know you don't know about the legendary Walttana. You know he has the legendary and powerful Walttriger, Lightning Walttriger." Yukki, the king of Lightning country, said, "I know about that, I think you told me Lightning Blade is dangerous and legendary." At that time, Lightning Blade easily killed the king of the Lighting Country. That time white nail became scared...

Have a love for that girl, but the Lord's Lightning Blade didn't ask that girl. The Lord's Lightning Blade said, "That girl." White nail came at the time. White asks the lord to light the Blade. "What happened, Blade?" Lord Lightning Blade didn't say any words against the question. Shizxavo asks, "Lord Lightning Blade, have a love against a strange girl?" White nail suddenly asked, "Who is that strange girl? No, no, that's my queen."

Lord Lighting Blade says to White nail, "What do you want Blade? Give much more items to people for free." White nail correctly asks the word of Lord Lighting Blade to Kinsvouyter. Kinsvouyter is a group of rich people; they give food items and other items to poor people for reds. Reds means cash. But Lord Lighting Blade gives these items for free. Then in the evening, White nail, Shizxavo, and Lord Lighting Blade go to the Cherry Blossom Tree Yard in Tuzuki in Lighting Country. Yard means a park. Tuzuki is a place in Lighting Country. Lord Lighting Blade asks some things to Shizxavo. White nail goes to buy

Some snack to Lord Lighting Blade and

Shizxavo. Then a few minutes later Lord Lighting Blade sees a beautiful girl. Shizxavo and White Nail became vanished. That girl came and stood in front of Lord Lighting Blade and asked in Japanese, "kimi no na wa" means "your name." At that time, Lord Lighting Blade felt aijo no kimochi [which means feelings of love] and Lord Lighting Blade gave the answer to the question, "My name is Lighting Blade Outsuki." At that time, the girl suddenly asked, "Are you related to the legend Lord Outsuki?" Lord Lighting Blade asked, "Yes. That's my grandpa." The girl also asked, "You're so lucky," but then suddenly Shizxavo asked, "You! What the hell are you talking about?" White Nail suddenly said, "Shut up, you monkey head. Do you know who she is? That is the new queen of the Lighting Country." Shizxavo asked, "What, Lord Lighting Blade has a love interest in that crazy girl?" White Nail became angry and said, "Why are you calling the girl crazy? She called our Lord Lighting Blade 'yours'!" White Nail didn't say any more words. Then the girl went to his house. Lord Lighting Blade came and drank some water. White Nail and Shizxavo taught some knowledge about

Aijo no kimochi. Next day the Lord Lighting Blade asks the name of that girl. That said his name. The name of that girl is Sakura, which means aaa... I don't know about it. It means I didn't know about the meaning of that name Sakura. You can find it yourself. That girl has a hobby. He writes one day in a diary. The diary is about the life of that girl, Sakura. One day Lord Lighting Blade has a dream to read the diary of Sakura. Lord Lighting Blade, his lightning Walttriger, and summon Shizxavo. And Lord Lighting Blade asked to pick the diary of Sakura when she was asleep. Shizxavo goes to the home of Sakura and picks the diary of Sakura and gives it to the Lord Lighting Blade. The Lord Lighting Blade reads the diary of Sakura. The lord's lighting blade became emotional. The Lord Lighting Blade reads a serious secret of Sakura. The Lord Lighting Blade takes a pen and writes on a page.

ANATA GA SUKI

"I am really sorry to disturb you, but do not play with the word Blade. Blade is only talking nonsense. And think you had only 22, and Blade also has 22." At that time, Sakura said, "He says he had only 24. He didn't know he was only 22." White nail goes to the place where Lord Lightning Blade is. Then Lord Lightning Blade asks White nail, "White nail, sense you're the only one hell in the world." White nail asked, "Yes, I am the only one hell in the world. You know, you only have 22! Now you think you have 22 in your training period. You know you'll practice in your future. That is my technique." Then Lord Lightning Blade and Sakura went, ate dinner, and went to Mount Fuji. Lord Lightning Blade and Sakura see a comet.

Chapter 37

The Death Days

The death of Sakura shocked the Lightning country and Lord Lightning Blade. Some memories of Sakura pierce the heart of the Lord's Lightning Blade. Lord Lightning Blade uses recovery magic to restore the life of Sakura. But at the right time, White nail came and said, "Blade, I know you're going to recover Sakura. That is just a dream. You can't recover Sakura. You know White nail sense. I can't live with her. Sakura is in my heart, and I am going to die. Grandpa Outsuki, please help me."

Lord Lightning Blade became emotional. One day, Lord Lightning Blade asked White nail, "I am quitting." White nail suddenly asked, "You're the king of the Lightning country, and you have 2 dreams. The first dream is over. The first one became the king of lightning in the country, and that dream is over. The next dream is to find and recover Lord Outsuki. You have a dream. Your new mission is over. The mission is to find Lord Outsuki."

And forget Lord Lighting Blade makes his heart stronger. Blade, white nail, and Shizxavo gone to find the legendary Lord Outsuki. Then they went to the whole country to find the legendary Lord Outsuki. They went to the laxeus in the Water Country. You think who will control the Lighting Country? The clone of white nail. That clone will take care of the Lighting Country when anyone kills the clone white nail feel PAIN.

Lord Lightning Blade and Shizxavo jump into the hole of death. Blade touches the heart of Lord Outsuki, meaning the secret door of Lord Outsuki's secret base. The door opened, and Lord Lightning Blade walked into the room, then Shizxavo entered the door. Lord Lightning Blade sees the dress of Lord Outsuki. Lord Lightning Blade picks the legendary dress of Lord Outsuki and sees the legendary crown of Lord Outsuki. Lord Lightning Blade looks at his Walttana and sees a place to fix the crown of Lord Outsuki. Lord Lightning Blade fixes the crown in the Walttana. That is a beautiful view. Then Lord Lightning Blade's lightning Walttriger automatically opened. The blood of Lightning Blade.

From his eyes means lighting Walttriger. Lord Lighting Blade picks reserve double power when lighting blade attaches the crown in the Walttana. Lord Lighting Blade looks around in the secret house of Lord Outsuki. Lord Lighting Blade sees a legendary katana, and Lord Lighting Blade picks that katana. There was a letter under the katana. Lord Lighting Blade reads the letter. "You know I have 3 katana, and you only find 2 katana. Blade, you have to find the mega katana gone to find the third one. Oh no, the first one." Blade asked, "The first mega katana in the world. White nail sense, that katana's name is noo!!!!!!!!!!!!!!!!!!!!!!"

That is a big secret. Shizxavo helps to find the katana. They find a legendary box and Lord Lighting Blade tries to open it. Lord Lighting Blade becomes angry, so the Blade picks his Walttana AND CUTS THE BIG BOX INTO 2 pieces. Lord Lighting Blade sees the legendary katana and a letter. The letter asks, "Place your heart in my legendary katana." For some reason, Lord Lighting Blade becomes scared. Lord Lighting Blade picks his Walttana, but he didn't choose that way. "Shizxavo! Please pick my heart and join to the

“AAA”

SUDDENLY SHIZXAVO PICKED THE HEART OF LORD LIGHTING BLADE AND PLACED IT TO THE KATANA!!!

Lord Lightning Blade suddenly stopped his asking. Lord Lightning Blade picked the katana. That katana has 2 lightning walttriggers with 10 dots, and he came from the hole of death. Lord Lightning Blade cried. The reason for that activity is Lord Lightning Blade thinking about the precious movements against Sakura. Lord Lightning Blade wiped his tears. White nail asked, "What about Lord Outsuki? I got 2 katana. The one is more precious than Walttana. I give my heart to that katana," Lightning Blade asked too White nail. White nail asked, "You talk about the lightning ten-dot Walttriger katana? Yes, Lord Lightning Blade talked about that katana." Now Lord Lightning Blade became a king like Lord Outsuki.

The seller is land. And Lord Lighting Blade, the sealer, is. White nail gets a map under the banyan tree. Shizxavo finds a map under the banyan tree. Lord Lighting Blade finds a map under the banyan tree. Lord Lighting Blade, Shizxavo, asked, "I found a map under the banyan tree," and they went to the home of Yukki. Lord Lighting Blade attaches all the maps. They find a place called the Mega Lighting Island. Lord Lighting Blade suddenly asked, "Order a ship, sensei!" Suddenly then the ship came. Lord Lighting Blade releases Shizxavo from Lightning Waltrigger. And now White nail, Shizxavo, and Lord Lighting Blade. The ship went to the Mega Lighting Island. At 8:22 that night, they reached the Mega Lighting Island. Shizxavo became shocked. The reason for that shock is that Lord Outsuki has a banyan tree. Shizxavo sees the banyan tree in the Mega Lighting Islands. Lord Lighting Blade goes to find the details about Lord Outsuki. White

Nail search under the banyan tree. Shizxavo gets information under the banyan tree. Lord Lighting Blade reads the letter picked under the banyan tree. "Find me under the tweltho Blade." Tweltho is the name of the banyan tree. White nail asked, "Lord Outsuki calls this banyan tree tweltho." Lord Lighting Blade asked how to go under the banyan. Shizxavo said, "I will take care of you." Shizxavo holds Lord Lighting Blade and White nail and goes to the legendary place in the universe. Lord Lighting Blade thinks about the movement against Sakura. Lord Lighting Blade becomes emotional and cries. Lord Lighting Blade sees the coffin of the legendary Lord Outsuki, but there was no coffin. That is the coffin of Sakura. Lord Lighting Blade relives the crazy smile. Lord Lighting Blade opens the coffin of Lord Outsuki. Lord Lighting Blade uses magic to recover the legendary Lord Outsuki. White nail suddenly calls the Queen of Nature Country. I talk about Raiyee Rock. In a few hours, Lord Raiyee Rock comes and looks at Lord Outsuki. Lord Outsuki holds the face of Lord lighting and says.

1	2	3
“You’re	The	New
King country.	of	my

Now I call You as Lord Lightning

Blade.

I Love You My

Dear.”

A new devil kills the legendary Lord Lightning Blade. At that time, the Lord Lightning Blade asked, "Grandpa, you're also in my heart. I love you so much. This is the last moment of mine on Earth. Please give me 'again'."

White nail and Shizxavo were shocked when the Lord's Lightning Blade fell onto the floor. Lord Outsuki also was shocked and emotional. Lord Outsuki and Raiyee Rock recovered Sakura. Sakura sees the legendary Lord's Lightning Blade. She became emotional and asked

"My heart Blade woke up."

Legendary Coming of

Goro Katzuyi

The fire

Goro Katzuyi The Legend Devil

Is coming for The Legendary

Lighting waltrigger Of lord

Lighting blade

Chapter 38

The Coming of the Legend

Then they think about what's next. That time a boy came in that place and said-

"Anata O

Koroshite Moidesu ka."

That time, Lord Outsuki asked, "We didn't know Japanese. But I know," Shizxavo said. "He asked for permission to kill Lord Outsuki in his dream," White nail asked, and that boy said, "Watashi WA Katzuyi Goro." Lord Outsuki used his power to go to the Liberian world. Then they went to the world of god. They saw the god of nature. Nature said to destroy Earth, and they shifted all the people to another world. They went to another world called Earth. That planet had many countries. They went to Japan. Lord White Nail married Raiyee Rock, and Lord Lightning Blade married Sakura. Lord Outsuki, Lord Lightning Blade, Sakura, Shizxavo, White nail, and Raiyee Rock lived there blissfully. But the devil came, Goro Katzuyi. Goro fought with Lord Lightning Blade. In that fight, Lord Lightning Blade opened his Lightning Waltrigger and Shizxavo. That was a beautiful view. But Goro picked one of the Waltriggers of Lord Lightning Blade. In that fight, every warrior joined, but Goro defeated all of them.

Chapter 39

The First Sense of Lord Lighting Blade

Haruto, the sixth leader of the Jyro sub-country, Jyro is a planet. Now, Haruto is going to the house of King Blaze, the king of Jyro. Haruto asked, "Lord Lighting Blade is in danger. Lord Lighting Blaze, go to see the Lord Lighting Blade. Kazoo, I am going to protect my son, Lord Lighting Blade," Lord Lighting Blaze went to see Lord Lighting Blade. Haruto, Syymaki, and Lighting Blaze. Lighting Blaze continued his way, but Haruto Syymaki stopped his way to drink water, but Lighting Blaze didn't stop his way.

Chapter 40

The First Sense of Lord Lighting Blade

Haruto is the sixth leader of the Jyro sub-country. Jyro is a planet. Now, Haruto is going to the house of King Blaze, the king of Jyro. Haruto asked, "Lord Lighting Blade is in danger. Lord Lighting Blaze, go to see the Lord Lighting Blade."

"Kazoki, I am going to protect my son, Lord Lighting Blade," Lord Lighting Blaze went to see Lord Lighting Blade. Haruto, Syymaki, and Lighting Blaze. Lighting Blaze continues his way, but Haruto Syymaki stops his way to drink water. Lighting Blaze doesn't stop his way. Then Lord Lighting Blaze reached Earth. Lord Lighting Outsuki became shocked and asked, "Lighting Blade, your father is coming." Lord Lighting Blade became shocked, and Goro stopped the fight to look at Lord Lighting Blade and Lord Lighting Blaze. Then Lord Lighting Blaze joined the fight, and they became a group. They opened their neutral. Lord Lighting Outsuki opened his kaiju. Lord Lighting Blade opened his new neutral, Yurei, and Lord Lighting Blaze opened his Yokai. But Goro also asked.

Lord Lightning Blade, Lord Lightning Blaze, and Lord Lightning Otsuki start the war, but Goro easily defects Lord Lightning Blade, Lord Lightning Blaze, and Lord Lightning Otsuki. The Lord's Lightning Blade easily goes to another planet, becoming stronger like Goro Katzuyi. But on Earth, Lord Otsuki goes to find Lord Lightning Blade.

This is the end.

Then Lord Lightning Blade to the god's planet. Lord Lightning Blade sees the Lightning God. Lord Lightning Blade asks Lightning God about his problems. Lightning God asked, "Lightning Blade, you're the best king of the Lightning country after Outsuki. And you're the son of Lord Lightning King Blaze Outsuki. Think about that. I gave it to you. My powers, but a problem: you can't kill that devil with your power or my power. That is so. Mix my power with your power and become powerful. Now you can fly; you can use lightning in fire and lightning dragon ball, then highlighting ball, lightning x lightning ball, neutral soul attack and so on. And he is so powerful. Kajakodaki's soul came, and he gave all his power to the Lord's Lightning Blade. Lord Lightning Blaze came and gave all his power to the Lord Lightning Blade. White nail Raiyee Rock gives their half soul to Lord Lightning Blade to go for training, and I know one day he will become powerful.

Years later.

Now, Goro is the leader of the Lighting Country. White nail killed by Gorokatzuyi.

Chapter 41

The Death of

Lord Lightning Blade goes to his world to defeat the devil, Goro Katzuyi. And the Lord Lightning Blade sees the people in the country of lightning. Lord Lightning Blade sees the legendary devil.

Goro Katzuyi

Came to go to the past of Goro Katzuyi.

Ten years Goro's real name is Shuyino. In his 10 years, his father dies. In his birth, his mother dies. His mother is unknown. His father is Umai Katzuyi. Umai means good, but he is not good. He kills poor girls, cuts them into 2 pieces, and puts them into the fell lake. That lake is known as the meat of girls. There are 12035 girls there. Goro has a sister. He kills his sister. And Goro's first enemy is his father. His sister's name is Nozomi. Goro loved

She is a sister. I know the pain of Goro. Nozomi's last year is 14. At that time, Goro was only 10. When he was 10 years old, he killed his father and cut into 9087 pieces and put them into that lake. Twenty years passed, and he was in love. His crush's name is Hinata Blue Crystal. But in the mission, blood kills Hinata. But Goro easily kills blood. Now, the fight vs. Katzuyi Goro and Lightning Blade has started.

Chapter 42

The Fight

This is the last.

And this is the first.

The mega war has started.

Lord Lightning Blade meets Goro Katsuyi.

The war started between

!!!!!!!!!!!!!!!!!!!!!!!!!!!!!!!!!

!!!!!!!!!!!!!!!!!!!!!!!!!!!!!!!!!

!!!!!!!!!

Lord Lighting Blade vs

GORO KATZUYI

spoiler alert

The

Mega War Is

started

"Welcome, Lord Lighting Blade," Goro Katayuki asked. "GORO, THIS IS THE LAST MOVEMENT OF YOU. YOU KNOW. CAME AND FIGHT WITH." Lord Lightning Blade asked, "OK. ANATA O KOROSHITE Lightning Blade DIDN'T ASK ANYTHING."

LORD LIGHTING BLADE AND

GORO KATZUYI GONE TO FIGHT. GORO GONE TO BEAT IN THE STOMACH OF Lord Lightning Blade AND. THAT TIME, GORO ASKED, "WATASHI WA KATZUYI GORO," BUT THAT TIME, Lord Lightning Blade ASKED. "WATASHI WA Lord Lightning Blade" THAT TIME, Lord Lightning Blade EASILY BEAT IN THE FACE OF GORO KATZUYI. GORO FELL TO THE FLOOR. THE TIME GORO THINK Lord Lightning Blade

EASILY DEFECT GORO. GORO

ASKED, "I AM FORGETTING LIGHTING BLADE IS THE UNIVERSE KING," Lord Lighting Blade ASKED, "SAYONARA, Lord Lighting Blade. BEAT IN THE HEAD OF GORO. GORO HEAD BECAME."

!!

!!

!! BOOO OOOOOOOO OOOOOOOM!!!!!!!!!!!!!!!!

!!

!!

!!!!!!!!!!!!!!!!

LORD LIGHTING BLADE PICK THE

ORGANS OF GORO AND DESTROY IT. LORD LIGHTING BLADE GONE FROM THAT PLACE. YOU KNOW THAT IS ONLY A CLONE OF GORO

CONTINUE

THIS WAR IS CONTINUING. LORD LIGHTING BLADE. IS COMING FOR...

Jimmy jayan

I am jimmy jayan. I am study in 7th at govt. Hs vazhamuttom.In Trivandrum black vs. white is my first story. Black and white has 2 parts. Black and white who will win this war is the first story of mine. I bore in 21 / 7 / 2012. My father's name is jayachandran. My mother's name is geethu. My hobbies are reading and writing.

may each day of my life became brighter

with the sunshine of sun and each moment

be filled with the heart of writing.

Jimmy Jayan

www.ingramcontent.com/pod-product-compliance
Lightning Source LLC
LaVergne TN
LVHW091051150826
845673LV00002B/546

* 9 7 9 8 8 9 5 8 8 3 4 5 7 *